Cave Boy

Written by Jane Clarke
Illustrated by Valentina Pieralli

Collins

Who and what is in this story?

Listen and say 🎧

cave

bear

mammoth

Cave Boy

Dad

Dan

Dad says, "Let's go to the park."

Dan and Dad go to the park.

Dan goes up the climbing frame.

Cave Boy goes up a tall tree.

Dan can see a big boy in the slide.

Cave Boy swings from tree to tree.
The bear can't catch him!

Ugg!

Dan gives food to the ducks on the pond.

Cave Boy sees a big mammoth!

Dan rides home on Dad.

Cave Boy rides home on a mammoth!

Dan is home. His cat is happy.

Let's read *Cave Boy*.

Cave Boy is home.
His cat is happy, too!

Picture dictionary

Listen and repeat

bear

cave

climbing frame

mammoth

park

pond

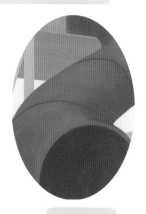

slide

swing

1 Look and order the story

2 Listen and say

Collins

Published by Collins
An imprint of HarperCollins*Publishers*
Westerhill Road
Bishopbriggs
Glasgow
G64 2QT

HarperCollins*Publishers*
1st Floor, Watermarque Building
Ringsend Road
Dublin 4
Ireland

William Collins' dream of knowledge for all began with the publication of his first book in 1819.

A self-educated mill worker, he not only enriched millions of lives, but also founded a flourishing publishing house. Today, staying true to this spirit, Collins books are packed with inspiration, innovation and practical expertise. They place you at the centre of a world of possibility and give you exactly what you need to explore it.

© HarperCollins*Publishers* Limited 2020

10 9 8 7 6 5 4 3 2

ISBN 978-0-00-839769-2

Collins® and COBUILD® are registered trademarks of HarperCollins*Publishers* Limited

www.collins.co.uk/elt

British Library Cataloguing in Publication Data

A catalogue record for this publication is available from the British Library.

Author: Jane Clarke
Illustrator: Valentina Pieralli (Beehive)
Series editor: Rebecca Adlard
Publishing manager: Lisa Todd
Product managers: Jennifer Hall and Caroline Green
In-house editor: Alma Puts Keren
Project manager: Emily Hooton
Editor: Tessie Papadopoulou-Dalton
Proofreaders: Natalie Murray and Michael Lamb
Cover designer: Kevin Robbins
Typesetter: 2Hoots Publishing Services Ltd
Audio produced by id audio, London
Reading guide author: Emma Wilkinson
Production controller: Rachel Weaver
Printed and bound by: GPS Group, Slovenia

Download the audio for this book and a reading guide for parents and teachers at www.collins.co.uk/839769